Peaceful Valley is a fun place
to visit, hope you enjoy it and come
back often!

Steven Jones
11/11/04

The Ballad of BLUE EAGLE

Written by:
Steven E. Jones

Illustrated by:
Steven E. Jones, Jr.

The Ballad of Blue Eagle

Cover Design by Steven E. Jones, Jr.

Printed and bound in Colombia by Imprelibros S.A.

ISBN:0-9747644-4-2

Published by:

Synergy Books

2525 W. Anderson Lane, Suite 540
Austin, Texas 78757

Tel: 512.407.8876
Fax: 512.478.2117
www.bookpros.com
www.blueeaglebooks.com

ACKNOWLEDGEMENT

These stories originated with my uncle, J. D. (Eb) Isaacks. He told these stories to his children in the evenings. My father adapted them to his style and told them for generations.

DEDICATION

This story is dedicated to the memory of my father, Harry R. Jones, whose many varied accomplishments, upon reflection, only grow in magnitude. He told these stories to his children and grandchildren as bedtime stories. It is hoped that this story might provide some insight into yet another side of this great man. To his family, he was "Blue Eagle."

- Steven E. Jones

There's a place way out beyond here and there,
Where critters can roam, with no people to care.

There're mountains and hilltops with a valley between,
And a river the likes of which you've never seen.

Evildoers in this place seldom ever dally.
They're not welcome you see - it's called Peaceful Valley.

This valley's safeguarded by one royal and regal;
To both friend and foe, he's known as
Blue Eagle!

Blue Eagle can soar above you so high.
He'll appear as no more than a speck in the sky.

With eyes so keen, from up high in the air,
He can still count your fingers, see the part
in your hair.

His wings tip-to-tip
measure just about twenty.
Speed and quickness,
he has them and plenty.

His talons, what power, but to be more concise,
When he grabs you it feels like the grip of a vise!

Each animal in the valley knows him on sight.
They follow his lead and respect his might.

"Do unto others," has
always been his creed.
To stay in the valley, this
word you must heed.

His friends they are many, but to name just a few:
There's Arny Armadillo and Pete Rabbit, too.

There's Timber the Beaver and Rio Raccoon
And ol' Toby Turple, who never comes soon.

We've Winston the Weasel and Boulder the Buck,
Petula Porcupine and old Daniel Duck.

Hal, the wise Owl and a
skunk named Laverne,
And Otto the Otter, with
mischief to burn.

Grady the Groundhog, who lives in a hole,
And mostly unseen is Mortimer Mole.

Jiffy the Jaybird and Charlotte the Shrew
And little Chip Munk, who can fit in your shoe.

There's Sammy the Squirrel and Tango the Snake,
Whose doubtful behavior is all Blue can take.

Sorry to give these
names in such a cluster,
But let's not forget
a bear that's named Buster.

Now if you will continue
to read 'till it ends,
You'll find out much more
about Blue and his friends.

Chapter I.
CLUGAR, THE CARNIVOROUS COUGAR

Peaceful Valley was near a mountain range, you see,
And there, mean animals often might be.

One of the meanest ever in these parts
Was a Cougar named Clugar; the name chills your hearts.

Clugar was always a nasty old fiend,
And the older he got, the more wicked
he seemed.

Most animals from
this place had long ago run,
Because Clugar would chase
them, if only for fun.

So Clugar decided
one night he would roam
Into the valley that Blue
Eagle called home.

Yes, to Peaceful Valley, this
vicious cat did sneak
To prey on the small ones,
for they were so weak.

In the dark of the night,
when all were asleep,
He got there quite late, for
all night he did creep.

Tired from his journey,
he decided to rest
And wait for the morning
when he'd be at his best.

Chapter II.

Morning came to this valley in such a nice way;
Peeking over the hills, through the trees, came the day.

Pete Rabbit would wake up
just before dawn,
To nibble in his garden
and work on his lawn.

Pete liked to rise
so early in the day
To do his chores first
so the others could say:

"Our friend Pete is a funny little rabbit.
To do things first is always his habit.
He can run so fast from there to here...
And go back again, before you can cheer.
With a nose he can wiggle and ears that flop
And feet so big, on a dime he'll stop.
He loves winning races and the games we play,
And whenever he's playing you can hear him say:
'Oh! I'm gonna win, gonna win by sally,
'Cause I'm the very best
in this great big valley!"

By now the sun was
pretty high in the sky,
And Pete knew his friends
would soon be coming by.

It was not unusual for this time of the week
For friends to drop by to play "Sneak and Peek."

His friend Sammy Squirrel was the first one to show,
Said he'd passed Toby Turple, "My goodness! How slow!"

Then came Laverne,
who prissed in from the right,
Looking quite charming
in her black and white.

Arny Armadillo
bumped into a tree,
Then wandered over,
so near-sighted is he.

Finally, ol' Toby came strolling on in.
Sammy looked up and asked, "Where have you been?"

"Hasty makes wasty," he said with a yawn,
"Let's get the game started before the day's gone."

Not so much different
was this game "Sneak and Peek"
From one you all know that's called "Hide and Seek."

This game was for learning and not just for pleasure.
Their ability to hide was important to measure.

For each animal in the forest, Mother Nature provides
Coloring that blends in wherever he hides.

The thing that's important for our friends to discover,
Is which surroundings fit best with his special color.

Blending colors is not so easy for some;
What if you're purple, as Toby had become?

His being purple is no reason to worry.
It's 'cause he's a Turple,
but that's another story.

Pete was "it," so he promised not to peek,
While the others to their hiding spots did sneak.

Waiting for them to find good hiding places,
Pete closed his eyes and counted twenty paces.

Chapter III

Pete finally yelled, "Here I come, ready or not!
All you critters had better stay in your spot!"

As he started to search, at the very same time,
Pete heard a noise that sent chills down his spine.

"Grroowell!" screamed Clugar, leaping from the bushes.
Pete dips and then darts, while on Clugar rushes.

Pete started left, then jumped right as he fled.
Clugar's legs got tangled and a tree hit his head.

"Help!" cried Sammy Squirrel
from up in that tree.
"Yeeow!" moaned Clugar, rubbing his head,
"What's this I see?"

"That rabbit's too fast and my head's in a whirl.
Since I'm so dizzy, I'll catch me a squirrel."

Clugar reached up
and started climbing that tree.
Sammy climbed out a limb
as far as could be.

Now Clugar slowly
crept out on that limb,
And little Sammy's chances
were looking quite slim.

Back on the ground,
Toby was talking to Pete.
"I think that mean cougar
wants Sammy to eat!

"This wicked behavior
is certainly illegal!
Our friend's only chance
is help from Blue Eagle!"

Pete started running like a bullet
through the thicket,

While Toby strolled over to talk to a cricket.

Then Toby turned and shouted out to Clugar,
"Leave him alone you vicious old cougar!"

Clugar just laughed
and the limb began to shake.
He could creep out no further
or it surely would break.

Toby yelled to Sammy to hold on so tight!
Sammy cried, "I am, with all of my might!"

If he were to fall from so high on that branch,
The fall would kill him. He didn't have a chance.

Just as Sammy's twigs
were breaking he could feel,
"KerWhump!" went Blue Eagle's
great talons of steel!

"Eeyoow!" screamed Clugar,
as he pawed at the air.
"This eagle has hold of my neck,
back and hair!"

Blue's wings stroked the air,
lifting ever higher,
And he talked to old Clugar,
who sure was a crier!

"You can't stay in this valley
with the rest of us
As long as your appetite
is so carnivorous."

"Let go of me," cried Clugar,
"you overstuffed crow!
That squirrel was my breakfast.
You ruined it, you know!"

"That's not all I've ruined,"
said Blue now so high,
"But I'll grant your request
and see if you can fly!"

Then Blue let go and the cougar started falling.
In just a few seconds, for Blue, he was calling.

"Help me! Please help me,
you big, beautiful bird!
If you save me, I'll listen
to your every word!"

Blue swiftly swooped in
before he hit the ground,
Grabbed Clugar by the tail
and turned him around.

"You're leaving this valley.
Your plan's run-a-muck.
If you ever come back,
you won't have such good luck!

"This valley is peaceful,
that much you should learn!
I'll take you home,
if you promise not to return."

Blue flew Clugar to the mountains he called home,
And Clugar kept promising never again to roam.

Back in the valley, Sammy was now on the ground,
And the other animals had gathered around.

Except for Pete Rabbit, who had not returned,
And of Sammy's safety, he had not yet learned.

Pete was so sad for he feared that his friend,
Without Blue Eagle's help, had come to his end.

While hopping through the woods, Pete started to cry,
"If that cougar got Sammy, I think I'll just die!"

Pete mournfully returned, only to hear - a cheer!
"Hurrah for Pete Rabbit! He sent Blue Eagle here!"

"Thank you, Pete, thank you!" Sammy said, "you're the best!"
Pete dried his eyes and got happy with the rest.

Although Pete was puzzled, he couldn't miss the chance
To join the celebration and do a little dance.

Very soon Blue Eagle
returned just to check,
To find if his timing
had spared Sammy's neck.

Sammy thanked Blue and
as Blue was leaving, he said,
"Be sure to thank Toby,
he really used his head."

Sammy was confused, but how could he know?
He had always teased Toby for being so slow!

Sammy said, "Toby, tell us, and please tell us true,
What is it you did to get word through to Blue?"

"I'll tell you my friends, if my words you will heed,
Just how much you're missing because of your speed.

"Pete Rabbit is fast but not faster than sound.
I talked to a cricket, 'stead of running around.

"Crickets usually don't chirp during the day.
He chirped for help and it
passed on that way."

"Blue heard of the trouble and came right along.
The rest of my words, I'll sing in this song:"

TOBY'S TUNE

"Some are brown, some are green. Yes, they're different from me.
No, I'm not one of those. I am purple you see.
Don't complain, use my brain, and I love being me.

Some rush here, then rush there; think what they never see.
Slow it down, take your time, see the wonders that be.
I have found, slowing down, you enjoy being free.

Chase a worm, race a snail, or just watch the grass grow.
These are some things you'll miss, just by hurrying so.
Quit that race, change your pace, you'll be happy, I know...
You'll be happy, I know..."

"You'll be happy, I know."

THE END

Toby's Tune

1. Some are brown, some are green. Yes, they're diff - erent from me.
2. Some rush here, then rush there; think what they nev - er see.
3. Chase a worm, race a snail, or just watch the grass grow.

1. No, I'm not one of those. I am pur - ple you see.
2. Slow it down, take your time, see the won - ders that be.
3. These are some things you'll miss, just by hur - ry - ing so.

1. Don't com - plain, use my brain, and I love be - ing me.
2. I have found, slow - ing down, you en - joy be - ing free.
3. Quit that race, change your pace, you'll be hap - py, I know...

you'll be hap - py, I know...

you'll be hap - py, I know.

Want to learn more about Blue Eagle and his friends?
Visit blueeaglebooks.com! Explore the world of
Peaceful Valley, and the animals that live there.

*The adventures continue
at www.blueeaglebooks.com!*